Mr. Teddy's Journey

Timothy Allen

Timothy Allen (signature)

Illustrated by Rosemary Williams

Mr. Teddy's Journey

Mr. Teddy's Journey

ISBN: 1500682306

This book is dedicated to my late father, J.H. Allen, Jr., who always believed in the magic of words; my mother, Opaline Allen, who has taught me that life is a continuous journey; and to the many children and adults with disabilities that I have been both privileged and blessed to have known.

Contents

Anna and Mr. T

Anna could not sit still. If one or both of her feet weren't kicking, her fingers were drumming on the table. If her hands and feet were still, her head seemed to twitch. She blinked a lot, not because her eyes were bothering her, but because she just couldn't help it. She had something wrong with her. She didn't know what it was, but she knew it had a letter name, something like "add", but that couldn't be right because that meant to put numbers together. Whatever it was, it wasn't good. Her mother was always telling her to sit still. Her teacher Mrs. Culver kept asking her to get the ants out of her pants. There weren't any ants in her pants that she knew of anyway. And it didn't matter how hard she tried, she just couldn't be still.

She didn't hate school, but she didn't like it either. None

of the kids wanted to be her friends because she was always moving, and always saying the wrong things. Sometimes she said things that she couldn't imagine herself saying, but she did, and then it was always too late to explain that she didn't mean it the way it sounded. Mrs. Culver tried to be nice to her, telling her to get herself under control, and then going back over things in class. It wasn't that she didn't listen to Mrs. Culver the first time she said them. It was just that she couldn't help but notice the blinds fluttering in the old windows on the yellow wall. She had to watch Emily as she twirled her hair. And that boy, Bob, seemed to be clicking his pencil against his desk again. Some days, the people going down the hall would catch her eye or a bug crawling across the tile floor in front of her seat. Some days, it was all a whirl and blur of things and motion and talk and lights and shadows and sounds, and before she knew it, she was on the bus headed home.

The only place that Anna really felt comfortable was in her bed at night with Mr. T, her teddy bear. Mr. T didn't seem to mind when she twisted and turned. He didn't look at her with disgust when she wiggled her feet or drummed her arms on the piles of covers. When she climbed into the soft folds of the daffodil coverlet her mother had bought for her pine knotted canopy bed, she drug in Mr. T by one arm. At night, she told Mr. T all about school, how Mindy spilled her tea in the cafeteria, and Joanie told Susan that Anna was always like a worm on a hot rock. Mr. T always listened. His big golden brown button eyes would shine in the light of the Daisy Duck lamp by her bed. His light brown fuzzy fur showed the prints of her hands or arms where she hugged him so tightly. There were spots on his back that were less fuzzy where she had brushed him too hard, while telling him about the new boy that asked if her batteries ever ran down. Mr. T never whimpered. He never complained. He liked Anna. She knew he did.

Anna couldn't remember when she and Mr. T first started their adventure. It seemed it might have been the night when she heard her mother telling her father that she had had it with Anna. Her constant wiggling and thumping and jumping and not listening were driving her crazy. Anna didn't hear the rest because she closed her door. In her red and blue socks and brown overalls she shuffled across the purple rug her grandmother had given her for her birthday, scooped Mr. T from the toy wagon that sat at the foot of her bed, and threw her body like a book bag full of books onto the field of daffodils.

It must have been that night. She didn't cry or sob. She kept clutching and unclutching Mr. T and saying to him that it was okay. She didn't know why she was always moving. It was a mystery like that story Mrs. Culver read in school one day. Well, if it was a mystery, then she and Mr. T would just have to be detectives like the boy and girl in the story. That was it. They would be detectives and find out why she couldn't be still.

3

When she turned off the lamp she pulled Mr. T up to her face, looked into his golden brown eyes and said, "You and I, Mr. T, are going to solve this mystery. We are going to find out why I can't be still. And when we find out why, then we'll know how to fix it. Now won't we, Mr. T? When we figure out the mystery, we'll fix it."

Mr. T looked at Anna. He didn't know what a mystery was. And he sure didn't know what it meant to be a detective; but as he looked at Anna with his brown button eyes, he willed love into the girl in constant motion. He wished his love could slow down the blur. If being a detective meant being a friend and helping, Mr. T was ready. And if it meant being a good listener, Mr. T was the best.

That night when Anna twisted and turned in her sleep and rolled over him, he didn't lose his breath. He didn't whimper or whine. He simply lay still and waited for Anna to awaken — ready to help her do whatever it took to solve this thing called a mystery. He stayed wide awake, eyes shining with love, ready to listen.

When Anna opened her eyes the next morning, she and Mr. T were woven into the bed of daffodils like a cocoon. They were wrapped so tightly that Mr. T's head seemed to bulge and his eyes were pushed out from his head.

"Well now, Mr. T," Anna said as she rolled out of the tangle and pulled the bear free, "it's time to get up. We have a mystery to solve."

As Anna skipped to the bathroom, she thought to herself,

4

"Now, where will we begin?" She peered into the large oval mirror over the sink as she set Mr. T on the towel rack.

"Where do we start?" she muttered as she saw the glimmer of the candle shaped lights on either side of the sink. "Maybe, right here," as she turned to look at the water dripping in the tub.

"What do you think, fuzzy friend?"

She knocked a comb and brush off the vanity. She stubbed her toe against the doorstop. Her elbow caught Mr. T and he tumbled to the pink tile floor.

"Why can't I be still, Mr. T?" Tears welled in her eyes as she bent to pick up her partner in the mystery.

All through her bath she thought and thought until she heard her mother call from the kitchen, "Anna, your breakfast is ready."

She thought as she dried herself and dressed. She knew that Mr. T was thinking too because he never took his eyes off of her. His little fuzzy ears, though shaken from the fall, were pointed and tall and listening.

When she bumped into the kitchen table and turned over her milk, her first clue appeared.

"Mother do you think that drinking milk makes me jumpy and jittery? Maybe, if I didn't drink milk, I could sit still."

"Don't be silly, Anna," her mother scolded as she wiped up the milk and rinsed the glass.

"Well, something is doing it, and Mr. T and I have decided

5

to solve the mystery."

Her mother stopped at the sink and turned slowly to face Anna. Her graying brown hair was damp from the steam in the sink. She wore a paisley blue housecoat. In her eyes were both a weariness and sadness rolled together like a peanut butter cookie.

"Honey, there's nothing that causes you to move so much. You just do."

Anna pulled Mr. T into her lap.

"Well, we think there is something, and because we don't know what, it must be a mystery, right? And if it is a mystery, then Mr. T and I are going to be detectives and solve it."

Anna's mother touched her shoulder as she walked past her. Anna wasn't sure, but she thought she was crying.

"Come on Mr. T!" she called in her firmest voice while she folded him under her left arm. "If it's not the milk, then maybe it's something else."

She barged through the screen door at the back of the kitchen. She knocked over the two trashcans by the door. She tripped over a rake that was leaning against the wall. When she caught her balance, she hopped down the driveway and twirled onto the sidewalk. She had Mr. T perched precariously under her arm. Even though dizzy from the twists and turns, he held on. Mr. T's thoughts swirled in his head from all the twists. A detective looks for clues, whatever they are. He looked as hard as he could all around him. His brown eyes reflected the sun. "Where are the clues to help Anna?" he thought. He watched and he listened.

Anna was hopping and turning and humming and jumping and skipping so much, she didn't really see where she was until she caught a glimpse in a twirling blur of a green wooden house with yellow shutters. It was her grandmother's house. When she stopped, she saw her grandmother sitting in the porch swing with a bag of beans and a large silver bowl in her lap.

"Grandmother!" she screamed as she danced up the steps to the porch. She turned over a pot of petunias. She kicked a pair of pruning sheers up to her grandmother's feet.

Her grandmother got up and set the beans and bowl down. As she picked up the pruning shears and turned the pot of petunias upright, she turned to Anna. She was wearing a bright red flowered apron. Her silver hair was pulled into a bun and held together by two blue butterflies.

"Why Anna and Mr. T!" she said, as she picked Anna and the bear up in her arms for a hug. She didn't hold them long, because Anna always wiggled so much that it made her grandmother nervous that she might drop her. She put her down on the gray wooden porch.

"What brings my sweet princess here today?"

Anna couldn't quit looking at the red flowers on her grandmother's apron. She thought she couldn't remember her grandmother ever not wearing an apron or butterflies in her hair. She looked down at her brown overalls and thought for a moment.

Then while she stood on one foot and swung the arm not holding Mr. T back and forth faster and faster, she said, "Mr. T and I are detectives out to solve a mystery. We are trying to figure out why I can't be still. And I think I may have just found a clue."

She looked smugly at Mr. T.

"Are you thinking what I'm thinking, Mr. T?" Mr. T's brown eyes shone with wonder.

"Grandmother, do you think clothes could make you twitchy and jumpy? I wear these overalls all the time. After all, they are my favorite things to wear and I've had them forever. So, if I'm always jumpy, do you think the overalls could be the reason?"

Anna rocked back and forth, tossing Mr. T into the air, but he didn't look worried that she would drop him. He was listening too hard to hear her grandmother's answer.

Anna's grandmother shook her head and sucked air through her false teeth making a funny little whistling sound. Anna knew they were false because she had taken them out once and let her look at them.

"Baby, clothes can't make you move all the time. Although I did have a wool suit one time that made me a little on edge every time that I wore it. But no sweetie, your overalls aren't keeping you from being still."

Anna looked at her feet as she tapped them softly on the planks. She held Mr. T so low that his feet dragged across the floor.

"Well, something makes me move all the time and I've got to find out what it is so I can fix it."

"Anna," her grandmother said, taking Mr. T from her arms, "some people are just nervous or high strung. They can't help it."

She patted Mr. T on the head and then began to stroke Anna's hair.

"You're right about one thing though. It is a mystery and mysteries can be fun. Being detectives can be fun, too. You know what? Your grandfather told me he liked to solve mysteries when he was a boy."

Anna didn't really remember her grandfather, since he had been gone so long.

"Wait right here," she said as a strange look crossed her face like she had seen Anna's grandfather standing on the edge of the porch.

She went into the house and Anna could hear her opening drawers and closet doors and the sound of her grandmother's voice muttering to herself, "Now where is it...here it is, I knew it was here somewhere."

Then she headed back out of the door onto the porch, and in her right hand was a moth eaten brown wool hat. It was a strange looking hat because it had two brims, one on either side, and two ears that seemed to be tied on top by a chocolate colored ribbon.

"This is a genuine detective hat that your grandfather used to wear when he was a boy and solving mysteries. Maybe this will help you solve yours."

She put the hat on Anna's head, but it was too small. Before Anna could grab it in frustration and anger and throw it off the porch, her grandmother took the hat and said, "Well, maybe this is meant for your detective partner here, Mr. T."

She put the hat on the bear's head and it just fit. Somehow, it made Mr. T look older. Somehow, it made his brown button eyes look wiser. Mr. T wished he could see himself. He bet he was one sharp bear in his new hat. Anna grabbed the bear and hugged him. She hugged her grandmother three times and danced in a circle.

"Thank you grandmother," she chirped as she jumped from step to step off the porch.

She kicked her feet as high as she could as she danced to the sidewalk.

"We've got a mystery to solve. Mr. T and I have a mystery to solve."

Mr. T bounced hard against Anna's side. He could barely see out from under the brim of the detective hat. He could barely breathe from being held so tightly. Somehow, he felt smarter in his new hat. In his eyes was not only love for Anna, but also a new understanding. He could help Anna solve her mystery. He could help her by just watching, and more importantly, by listening.

As Anna turned to cross the street, she tripped and fell off the curb. When she stood up she saw a bloody patch on her right knee.

"Another scrape," Anna thought.

She had had a thousand scrapes and bruises. She was always falling or bumping into something, and every time she went home her mother would shake her head. As she cleaned and doctored the wounds she would mutter, "Anna, Anna, what are we going to do with you?"

It had happened so often that at one time Anna thought her name might have doubled. She reached down and wiped off the blood and dirt. She picked up Mr. T and put his hat back on his head.

"Mr. T, this little wound is not going to stop good detectives like you and me," and she hopscotched down the side of the street until she got to the park.

The park at the end of Jacobs Street was Anna's favorite place in the world. She came there every day after school and on weekends when it wasn't raining. She nestled herself against the trunk of a poplar tree and balanced Mr. T on her knees.

"Well Mr. T, what we need is another clue. Don't we old bear?"

Mr. T looked at Anna from under the brim of his hat. Light shimmered in his eyes as the sun filtered through the leaves of the tree. The breeze felt good to Anna and Mr. T. It felt good just to listen.

Across the park in a large grassy clearing, Anna could hear and see a large group of children kicking a ball back and forth. Anna wanted to join them, but she knew it wouldn't work. She had tried it before. She always knocked someone down or tripped or said something silly that made someone mad. She recognized most of the children and she knew they saw her because they pointed her way. But no one asked her over or called her name. "That's okay, isn't it, Mr. T? After all we don't have time for games. We have a mystery to solve."

Anna hadn't noticed the hole she had dug with her feet as she scraped her tennis shoes back and forth, back and forth, while she talked.

"So, it's not the milk, and it's not my overalls, Mr. T. What could it be that is making me move all the time? It has to be something that I do everyday."

And then it dawned on her, another clue.

Just then, a familiar voice sounded from behind Anna.

"Hello, Anna. What a pretty day to be in the park. And who do you have with you? What a strange hat."

Anna looked up, and through the glare of the sun, she saw a pretty dark haired lady in a purple dress and white sandals.

"Hello, Mrs. Johnson. This is Mr. T, and he's not wearing a strange hat. It's a detective hat. We are out to solve a mystery."

Mrs. Johnson lived just down the street from Anna. She had a daughter named Priscilla who was in Anna's grade at school. When they had first moved onto the block, Mrs. Johnson and Priscilla had come over to visit a couple of times, but it didn't work out because Priscilla said that Anna made her nervous and she was always saying weird things.

Now Priscilla would barely speak to Anna at school.

"A mystery, that's interesting. What kind of mystery are you and your bear trying to solve?"

"We're trying to find out why I move all the time, Mrs. Johnson, and I think I may have just discovered an important clue. You see, I come to this park almost every day, and everyday I can't seem to be still. Do you think that a place like the park could be what is making me move all the time?"

Mrs. Johnson held her hand up to shield her eyes from the sun. Anna couldn't take her eyes off the ring on Mrs. Johnson's finger. It kept casting glimmers and sparkles all over the ground. Anna started rolling her feet over a stick and thumping her left hand against the tree trunk.

"Anna," Mrs. Johnson's forehead wrinkled and her eyes narrowed, "honey, a place can't make you move all the time. That's just the way some people are. You're just a little nervous that's all. Have you seen Priscilla?"

Mrs. Johnson looked eager to change the subject.

"She's over there." Anna pointed to the big grassy area. Mrs. Johnson started across the park and then stopped and turned to face Anna.

"You just need to calm down a little, Anna, that's all. Just, calm down a little." And then she turned and walked away. The breeze caught her purple dress and it seemed to billow like a sail on the bright blue sky.

"Calm down a little," Anna thought, "I can't just calm down a little." She jumped up with Mr. T's legs on either side of her head.

"Well, Mr. T, if it isn't the park then it must be something else and good detectives don't give up so easily."

She ran right into the trunk of the tree as she turned to go, but she held onto Mr. T. Though he bobbled and jiggled as Anna spun like a top on her way home, he still held on tight. He didn't know how the hat stayed on his head. Sometimes, he felt like his head would bounce off. But he loved this little girl that spun like a top. He wanted more than anything else to help her. And as Anna whistled and laughed and sang and talked, Mr. T listened like a good detective.

When Anna barreled through the front door of her house, her mother was waiting in the living room with her father. She said, "Anna, Anna," as Anna could have predicted because she had a bloody scrape on her knee, a knot on her head, and scratches that she didn't even remember getting. As her mother cleaned her wounds in the bathroom, she said, "Anna, we have something we want you to try. The doctor says it may help you not move so much."

Anna could remember being at the doctor's one day, but didn't remember much else except bright lights and lots of white and what seemed like thousands of voices and a hundred questions and pricks and pokes. Her mother put a little white pill in Anna's mouth and gave her a glass of water to drink.

"The doctor thinks this may help you, Anna, if you take it twice a day."

"Will these pills solve the mystery?" Anna asked.

"We hope so, honey."

"Did you hear that, Mr. T? These little pills might be the solution to our mystery."

Mr. T's brown eyes seemed to show wonder at Anna's words. He watched her take the little pill. He didn't know how a pill could solve the mystery, but he hoped with all his fuzzy might that it would. He peered from underneath the brim of his detective hat to see if she looked different. He perked up his brown fuzzy ears to listen for every sound.

That night in bed, Anna still tossed and turned, and twisted herself and Mr. T into knots. And just before she finally went to sleep, she told Mr. T that she really didn't feel any different. As usual, Mr. T didn't complain or make noise or ignore her. He lay as close as he could in the cocoon that she wove. He lay very still, but he did not sleep. He wanted to be awake when she changed into a butterfly. His brown button eyes would catch the first unraveling of her wings. His little ears would hear their first flutter. When her movements settled and her wings unfolded, Mr. T wanted to catch it all. He wanted to see and hear everything.

The next morning, Anna still knocked things off the vanity in the bathroom and bumped Mr. T with her elbow, but she didn't seem to notice the water dripping in the tub. When she came down to breakfast and her mother gave her another little white pill, she told her she didn't feel any different. Her feet still kicked against the table non-stop, but she didn't spill her milk. That morning in church she still knocked the hymnal to the floor three times and tripped getting into the pew, but she did remember some of the songs they sang. That afternoon in the park when she and Mr. T leaned against the poplar tree, she didn't dig any holes with her feet, and she wasn't sure, but she thought she could actually follow the games the kids were playing in the park.

In the next few days Anna seemed to have accidents less and less. At school, she heard everything Mrs. Culver said and she made 100 on her spelling test. At recess, the new girl actually spoke to her and Anna didn't say anything dumb or stupid.

As the weeks went by, Anna quit taking Mr. T to bed with her. In her room she was either doing homework or talking to her friends on the phone or playing games with her friends right there on the field of daffodils on her bed. Mr. T sat on top of the toys in the wagon; his brown detective hat perched on his head. He had seen and heard it all. The shy little girl that couldn't be still had evolved into a beautiful little girl who had friends and the time to enjoy them. Things no longer passed in a whirl of motion and color. She had time to enjoy each minute and each thing.

Mr. T's eyes shone with the wonder of it all. He thought that a good detective must have a big heart because his seemed so large that it just might pop, it was so full of love! On his perch he sat, eyes wide and ears pointed. He didn't want to miss a thing. After all, Anna might somehow still need him. He sat very still and watched, and more than anything else he listened.

It was a Friday while Anna was at school that her mother decided to clean out her room. She found toys that Anna had not played with in years. She found Mr. T with the detective hat still atop his head. She couldn't remember the teddy bear in Anna's arms in months, so she packed him and the other toys into the box for her garage sale.

On Saturday morning when Anna came down for breakfast, her mother told her she was selling some of her old toys at the garage sale and that she needed to go through them to see if there were any she wanted to keep, but Anna didn't stop to look. She was in a hurry for a soccer game in the park with her friends.

Anna's mother was just about to load all the stuff that didn't sell back into the garage, when the old station wagon pulled into the driveway. A sad looking woman with long blonde hair got out with a small redheaded boy covered with freckles. He was hanging onto the back of her denim skirt.

"I was just about to close up, but you're welcome to look while I'm putting things into the boxes."

The woman smiled and turned to look at the table of toys. "Look at these, Henry. Do you see anything you like?"

When Henry peered from behind the folds of his mother's skirt, he saw a teddy bear with a very strange looking hat on his head, lying on his side at the end of the table. Henry didn't say anything, but he pointed at the bear.

"You want the teddy bear, Henry? Is that what you want?" Henry only nodded.

"How much do you want for this teddy bear?"

Anna's mother grinned. "It's yours if you want it," and she handed it to Henry.

Henry took the hat off the bear's head and started to hand it to Anna's mother.

"Oh no," she said, "the hat goes with the bear," and she put the hat back on the teddy bear's head.

After Henry's mother had strapped him into the back seat of the car and they were on their way home, she thought she could hear him whispering. When she looked in the rear view mirror, there was Henry in his seat with the bear perched on his lap. The strange hat made the bear look almost comical, but there was something about the bear's eyes. She couldn't quite hear what her son, with a very serious look on his face, was saying to the bear. But of one thing she was sure. The teddy bear wasn't just sitting there. He was gazing fondly at her son, and he seemed to be listening.

Henry and Mr. Bob

Henry didn't know how long his dad had been gone. He knew it was a long time. It had been at least two birthdays and one Christmas. He saw him then, not for very long, but he did see him. It always made him feel strange. He knew that he loved his dad, but he didn't feel comfortable with him anymore. At night he could still sometimes remember things they used to do or play, but more often he remembered his mom and dad fighting. Through his closed door he could hear them. From under his pillow he could hear them. He still got nervous at loud sounds because he always thought of the slamming doors and the heavy footsteps across the living room floor. He remembered his mother crying a lot. At night she would come into his room and pull him from under his covers and hold him tightly while sobbing that everything would be all right. She would cry so hard that the top of his head would get wet. In the mornings, he was never sure if it had happened or not, since his head was dry and there was no sign that his mother had been in his room.

Henry was not happy at school. He had not been happy even before his daddy left. He could not speak plainly. No matter how hard he tried, his r's sounded like w's, and when he became excited, it was hard to understand him at all. His mother said it was a stutter and the special teacher at the school said it was an "artic problem." He didn't know how that could be, since on TV they said that was where penguins and Eskimos lived. What could that have to do with the way he talked?

Whatever it was, he had learned to talk very little. The other kids laughed when he read. They laughed when he talked. The teachers kept asking him to repeat himself. And that special teacher kept putting peanut butter on the end of his tongue and making him try different sounds. As a result, he no longer liked peanut butter and jelly sandwiches.

He used to like baseball when his dad was around. But his mother didn't know much about it, and he didn't like her coming to games or practice because she seemed to baby him too much. So, he quit playing. He also knew his mother needed him too much for him to be away too long. He knew this because she told him every day that she didn't know how she would get along without her little man. Henry would just nod. It was easier not to talk. Most of the time, he stayed at home in his room, or in the backyard, or went places with his mother. He went everywhere with his mother, whether he liked it or not, because she needed him there.

So, after not talking for so long, on that first night in his racecar bed with his new teddy bear, he had a lot to say. Wearing his pro-baseball tee shirt and gym shorts, he climbed under the Mickey Mouse sheets. The teddy bear wearing the detective hat was lodged beneath his right arm. He pulled the covers up to his chin and set the bear on his chest.

"Well, here we are in my room. Is it like what you expected from what I told you in the car?"

The teddy bear's eyes seemed to take in the whole room while staring at Henry at the same time.

"It's not a bad place is it TTT Teddy?"

The teddy bear didn't even seem to wince or notice when Henry stuttered or forgot his r's.

"Do you mind if I call you Mr. Bob? That's my ddd dad's name and I used to talk to him a lot." Mr. Bob just sat on Henry's chest and didn't move. He seemed pleased with the name.

"I like your hat too, Mr. Bob," Henry reached to the shelf behind his bed and took down a New York Yankees' baseball cap and pulled it on his head.

"This is my favorite hat."

Two hatted shadows danced on the wall by the bed.

"I sure am glad you are here, MMMMr. Bob."

Mr. Bob didn't say anything but his eyes seemed to say that he was glad that he was there too. When Henry finally became too sleepy to talk, he turned out the baseball and glove lamp by his bed, and Mr. Bob was still sitting at attention and listening.

On Saturday when Henry came into the kitchen for breakfast, he had Mr. Bob hanging on his arm.

His mother turned, "Henry, I know you like your new teddy bear, but you don't have to bring him to the breakfast table." She set a bowl of frosted flakes on the table.

Henry sat down with Mr. Bob in his lap, "He's not just a teddy bear Mom, he's my friend and his name is Mr. Bob."

Tears filled his mother's eyes, "I don't know if that's a good name, Henry."

She brought the milk from the refrigerator.

"It's a perfectly good name, I think," said Henry with hardly a stutter in his voice. Mr. Bob just sat quietly looking out the kitchen window.

"Well, anyway, I guess it won't hurt. I called Margaret this morning and Charlie is coming over to play."

Charlie was a year younger than Henry and lived just a couple of streets over. At one time they had been good friends. That was when his dad was still there. Henry's mom and dad spent a lot of time with Charlie's parents, so Henry and Charlie were always thrown together. Charlie wasn't really mean to Henry. He only occasionally snickered at some of his mumbled words. They just didn't seem to like the same things.

"But, Mom, I was going to stay here with Mr. Bob and help you today." His r's seemed to disappear again.

"You spend too much time here, Henry. It's time for you to get out some. I'll be okay." She started wiping the brown tile on the kitchen counter top.

"Well, okay, but I'm going to take Mr. Bob with me."

Henry dropped his spoon in the bowl and with Mr. Bob in tow, raced out the kitchen door.

As he sat down on the concrete step at the edge of the porch, he held Mr. Bob up to his face. "Charlie's okay, Mr. Bob, but it's really going to be you and me. And we really need to stay close in case mom needs me."

Mr. Bob understood Henry even through his slurs and mumbles. He didn't snicker or make fun. He just listened.

Then up the driveway on a red Schwinn bicycle came a brown-haired boy with green eyes. He was wearing a red and white striped tee shirt and blue cut-off jeans. On his head was an Atlanta Braves' baseball hat. In his basket were a glove, ball and bat.

"Hey, Henry you wanta play some ball? What's with the bear? What a crazy looking hat!" Charlie jumped off his bike and let it fall into the yard at the side of the house. He reached down to get his glove and ball.

"The bear is Mr. Bob and his hat is a detective hat and it isn't crazy at all, not any crazier than your Braves' hat." Henry sat Mr. Bob on his shoulder.

"What'd you say?" Charlie looked baffled as he threw the ball into his glove.

Henry's speech became more garbled when he was upset or angry.

"You heard what I said." Henry stood and kicked a rock across the yard.

"Mr. Bob and I are going for a bike ride."

Henry went into the gray-shingled garage beside his house and came out pushing an old blue bike that had belonged to his father. He used a belt to strap Mr. Bob to the handlebars.

"Okay, let's go for a bike ride then. Maybe later we can play ball."

Charlie threw down his ball and glove and climbed on his bike, pushing his hat back farther on his head.

"I didn't say the bear was crazy, just his hat."

By then, Henry was already down the driveway turning on the sidewalk toward Miller's orchard at the edge of the subdivision where he lived.

"Mr. Bob," he whispered. "We're going to have a good time with or without Charlie. I want to show you my special place."

Miller's orchard was the only place besides school that Henry went without his mother. He loved the rows and rows of apple trees. He loved the smell of apples. When he rode his bike there, people working in the orchard knew who he was and would often wave. He could talk there all he wanted and it didn't matter how much he stuttered or slurred, no one heard or cared. He remembered coming there with his dad and picking apples. He remembered his dad carrying him on his shoulders or holding him up so he could get the best apple off the tree. He remembered laughing. He could still imagine his dad holding his hand as they walked.

"Wait up, Henry!" Charlie pulled up beside him breathing hard.

"Can I carry the bear, I mean Mr. Bob, awhile?"

"I don't know. Mr. Bob is new to bicycles and he's kind of nervous." Henry held Mr. Bob with his left hand.

"I'll be careful and he'll be more comfortable in my basket."

Henry thought for a minute and then untied Mr. Bob and handed him to Charlie.

"Mr. Bob, I guess it would be more comfortable in the basket instead of on this hard old handlebar."

Mr. Bob didn't seem to mind, not as long as he was still with Henry and close enough to listen.

The two boys wove in and out of the apple trees. Henry would chase Charlie. Then Charlie would race Henry from one end of the orchard to the other. They laughed and they whooped. Mr. Bob just bounced and bounced in the basket. His eyes shone like dark jewels from the pinpoints of sunlight that wove through the thick leaves of the old apple trees. Soon, the boys were so winded they climbed off of their bikes and lay against an old plow at the south end of the orchard. Henry, of course, took Mr. Bob and sat him on top of the plow like he might be about to finish his farming chores for the day. Mr. Bob seemed pleased not to be bouncing for a while. His eyes were wide and dark, and though tired, he was still listening.

"I'm sorry about your dad." Charlie picked up a small stick and began to poke a hole into the dirt.

"It's okay. My mom says it's for the best. And I still see him sometimes." A quiver entered Henry's voice along with the stutters and slurs.

"Well, my mom says it's a shame. She thinks your mom should get out more. And why did you quit the baseball team? If it was because they make fun, they were always kidding. They don't mean anything by it. Look at Joe, he has one blue eye and one brown one, and Mike is as fat as a cow and Tony can't even catch a ball."

"My mom needs me around a lot now. She cries and gets real sad and lonely."

"But she told my mom this morning that you needed to get out more."

"Well, I need to get back, I mean Mr. Bob and I need to get back and check on her." Henry plucked Mr. Bob from the plow and jumped on his bike.

Before Charlie could say anything else, Henry and Mr. Bob were already halfway through the orchard. When Charlie got to Henry's house to get his ball, bat and glove, Henry had already put his bike in the garage and he and Mr. Bob were in the house sitting on the bed in his room.

Though Charlie yelled for Henry, Henry whispered for Mr. Bob to be quiet.

"He is nice, Mr. Bob. But he doesn't understand that my mother needs us right now."

Henry laid Mr. Bob on the pillow beside him and began to tell him stories about him and his dad, about the times in the orchard, about how Mr. Bob would like him, about baseball games and tickle tag, and naps on his dad's lap on Sunday mornings.

As Henry fell asleep with a single tear glistening on the side of his face, Mr. Bob lay with his eyes wide open. He had not heard the w's for r's. He had not heard the stutters or slurs. He had understood every word. He would stay awake just in case Henry woke up and needed to talk again. Mr. Bob was a very good listener.

School was still a struggle for Henry. He stayed to himself and saw the special teacher every day. But he did see Charlie in the lunchroom and Charlie would wave to him. At first, Henry would just smile, but he finally started waving back. Most of what Henry did during the day was to commit to memory everything that happened. And when he got home he could tell Mr. Bob all about it. When he reached his house, Mr. Bob would be waiting anxiously on the shelf above Henry's bed, brown eyes sparkling with anticipation to hear all about Henry's day.

Henry would throw his books on his desk, and race for the bed where he would fling himself like a Frisbee. He would reach up and grab Mr. Bob, perch him on his chest, and begin to talk about how Joey Smith spit milk on the table, or Gracie Johnson tripped in the gym and knocked over the rack of soccer balls, or how Mrs. Williams didn't call on him once, or how the special teacher told him his r's were coming along.

Mr. Bob, as usual, sat at attention hanging on to every word. To Mr. Bob, Henry's words were perfect. To Mr. Bob, the stories Henry told were magical. Mr. Bob sat very still with love in his eyes and listened.

The next time Henry's mother told him Charlie was coming over to spend Saturday with him, Henry was actually kind of glad.

"Mr. Bob, you remember Charlie? He carried you in his basket. Maybe, we'll take a bike ride and just maybe we'll play a little ball." Mr. Bob's eyes filled with excitement just from the sound in Henry's voice.

So, when Charlie arrived that Saturday morning, Mr. Bob and Henry were sitting on the steps waiting. They took off for the orchard on their bikes. But this time Charlie didn't have to ask.

Henry said, "Do you reckon Mr. Bob could ride in your basket again, Charlie? He told me he was much more comfortable there."

Charlie smiled as he took Mr. Bob and sat him in his basket. They played the same chase games that they had before. Except when they settled down next to the old plow to rest, Charlie didn't bring up Henry's dad. Henry did.

"My dad's supposed to come see me tomorrow. He's bringing a girlfriend, if you can believe it. My mother cried a little last night, but she didn't come into my room. This morning she was quiet, but I think she still feels bad."

Charlie didn't say anything. It was as if he had taken lessons from Mr. Bob. He just sat and listened.

"Have you started baseball practice yet? Think we could toss a little when we get back to the house?"

Charlie just smiled and said, "Sure. I'll race you."

Then he grabbed Mr. Bob, slung him into his basket, and took off through the orchard with Henry laughing and following close behind him.

When the boys arrived at Henry's house, Charlie's mother was there. She and Henry's mother had a surprise for them in the backyard. They had set up the old tent that Henry's family had used when they went camping. That was when his dad was still there.

Charlie's mother beamed, "We thought you might like to camp out tonight."

Henry's mother said, "And that's not all," she held out two bundles of blue. "We have uniforms for you, and we've even got something for Mr. Bob."

The boys looked at each other. They ran up to Henry's room to put on the uniforms. When they came down, their mothers fastened their kerchiefs around their necks.

In Henry's mother's arms was Mr. Bob wearing his

detective hat and now a Cub Scout kerchief around his neck, beaming with pride. The boys raced for the tent with Mr. Bob hanging between their arms.

That night they sat and talked about their uniforms, ate marshmallows and hotdogs, and told scary stories until Mr. Bob seemed to get a little shaky. They caught fireflies, played tag in the dark among the shrubs in the backyard, and finally fell asleep under the old quilt in the tent with Mr. Bob snuggled between the two of them. Mr. Bob didn't sleep. He was too excited. He didn't know what it meant to be a Cub Scout, but it sounded like an adventure, and he was always ready for an adventure as long as it was with Henry and their new friend Charlie. So, he peeked over the quilt top in the quiet of the darkness and waited and listened.

The next morning when the boys and Mr. Bob went into the kitchen for breakfast, Henry was a little bit nervous about being a Cub Scout.

"Mother, I'm not so sure about the Cub Scout thing." He hung his head down and wouldn't look at Charlie or Mr. Bob. He seemed to be slurring and stuttering more.

"You know, I need to be around here to help you."

Henry's mother put two plates of pancakes in front of the boys. She had a strange far away look on her face.

"Nonsense, Henry, you know I always like for you to be around here, but this will be good for you. Besides, did I tell you who your scout leader was?" Three sets of eyes focused on her.

"It's your dad." Then Henry's mother went to the cabinet to get syrup for their pancakes.

Henry looked at Charlie. Then he took Mr. Bob in his arms and started crying before he could stop himself. Charlie just looked down at his pancakes. Mr. Bob just looked in wonder as he felt the top of his head get wet.

When Henry's dad arrived that morning, Henry was so excited about Charlie meeting his dad, about his dad meeting Mr. Bob, about the Cub Scouts, and with all the things that had happened on their campout swirling in his head, that he didn't pay much attention to the lady with his dad. And that night, when he and Mr. Bob were in bed and Henry was talking a mile a minute, he realized he didn't even remember what the lady looked like. But he did seem to remember that she was nice. Mr. Bob lay with his head on the other pillow, eyes focused on Henry, detective hat on his head, Cub Scout kerchief around his neck, tired and happy. He wasn't sure, but he didn't think Henry was slurring as much. Of course, that didn't matter anyway to Mr. Bob. He was too busy listening for more important things to notice.

The last few weeks of school went by quickly for Henry. He was talking more in class. He just had to stop and remind himself sometimes to be careful before he spoke, and soon he didn't have to remind himself at all. His w's seemed to be w's and his r's came out as r's, and unless he was excited or rushed, everyone understood him. There were Cub Scout meetings every week that meant he got to see his dad a lot. There were cookouts and camping and projects and lots of other boys that no longer made fun of Henry. He had even signed up to play baseball again that summer. At first, he took Mr. Bob with him everywhere and he worried about leaving his mother. But she seemed to be happy just from his being happy and he worried less and less. And he began to leave Mr. Bob behind more and more, sitting on his shelf, waiting for Henry to return, ready to listen.

Henry didn't notice that things were missing from his shelf when his mom put up his baseball trophy and Cub Scout projects. It wasn't until months later that he thought about Mr. Bob and asked her where he was. She told him that a lady at their church had a granddaughter that lived with her. The little girl didn't have any friends. She was kind of slow, a really special child. She hoped Henry didn't mind, but she had given Mr. Bob to her so that the little girl could have a friend. Henry wasn't upset at all. He was too busy with baseball and his friends. Besides, if the girl needed a friend, he did remember that Mr. Bob was the best. And if the little girl needed someone to talk to, there was nobody better. Mr. Bob was a good listener.

Gracie and Cookie Darling

Gracie was slow, not slow in that she moved slowly, although she didn't walk too fast. But she just didn't think too quickly. She knew her name was Gracie and she had finally remembered how to write it. She knew her family's names. But she had trouble remembering everybody else, and she often got them mixed up. She didn't have any friends because she couldn't play the games they liked to play. And rules didn't make sense for Gracie. The games seemed like fun, but she didn't understand them. The team she played on always lost and they blamed her. So, they quit asking her to play.

Gracie had two younger brothers and a little sister, but she didn't live with them. Her family was very poor, or so she had heard people say. She didn't know what the word poor meant, but she guessed it meant to be made fun of, since that was what she always remembered people doing.

Gracie lived with her grandmother, Mama Darling, in a little four-room house on the edge of town. She couldn't think of a time when she didn't live there, but she assumed she had lived with her parents at one time or another.

She usually saw her mama and daddy on Sundays. She knew it was on Sundays because that was when Mama Darling always cooked the big meal. That meal was always the best thing. The smells and the tastes she could remember.

Her brothers and sisters didn't say much to her when they were at Mama Darling's. They played games, watched TV, read books, or sat in their parents' laps. Gracie didn't sit in their laps. She was too big, her mama said. Her mama also always looked at her daddy and said, "Poor Gracie." That was another reason she knew she was poor.

Mama Darling told Gracie that Gracie lived there to keep her company. Gracie loved Mama Darling. Mama Darling was really old. She had snow white hair that was real wispy like cotton. She wore brown glasses that covered her green eyes. Her face was wrinkled like one of Gracie's dresses before Mama Darling ironed it. But she seemed to always keep one arm around Gracie, and she would click her tongue against her teeth, chuckle and say, "Now what do you think of that, Gracie?" Gracie chuckled too. She didn't really know what Mama Darling meant.

Mama Darling always wore either a light blue housedress

or a faded yellow one. If she was in the kitchen, she wore an apron covered with red roses. Gracie had her own apron that was white with little pink flowers.

Gracie didn't go to school where her brothers and sister went. She went to a very special school. Mama Darling said it was for very special people. Gracie thought it must be for kids that were real slow because the kids there seemed to be slower than she was. Some of them couldn't even talk. One boy sat in a chair all day. And this little girl with curly blonde hair lay on a mat with her thumb in her mouth.

Gracie spent most of her school day sitting at a table and looking at books. She really liked all the pictures. Her favorite times were when the pretty lady with the black hair sat down and looked at the books with her and told her stories about the pictures. Sometimes, they made her work on the letters in her name or they tried to make her count things. But she got the numbers all mixed up and someone would get mad and they would say, "Gracie, can't you remember anything?" After that, they would let her sit with her books for a long time.

When she would get off the little bus in front of her house in the afternoon, Mama Darling would be waiting in an old brown wooden chair on her porch and would say, "My little Gracie, sweet pea, did you have a good day at school?"

Then they would go into the kitchen, Mama Darling's arm wrapped around her, where she would eat a tomato sandwich and drink a glass of tea. She couldn't remember a lot about the school day to tell her, but what she did tell made Mama Darling click her tongue against her teeth and shake her head and chuckle.

At night she would sit in the living room on the old brown and green couch beside Mama Darling while some TV show was on, and she and Mama Darling would knit. Mama Darling said that Gracie was a natural with knitting needles. Gracie didn't know what that meant. She just knew she could move those needles and make things. Gracie couldn't count the stitches or ties, but if Mama Darling would show her how to do them once, and then tell her when to stop or when to start a new one, and then show her how again, Gracie could knit all night long. And she would if someone didn't tell her to stop and go to bed.

Gracie had made things to go around the necks of all of her family. She had even taken one to the black haired lady at school. For some reason, the black haired lady cried. But Mama Darling said it was maybe because she was so happy.

It was one of those nights when Gracie was knitting that her grandmother brought out the teddy bear.

She said, "Gracie, sweet pea, I've got a friend for you."

Gracie looked up from her needles and there was this fuzzy bear with a funny looking brown hat on his head and a yellow scarf tied around his neck. Gracie stared into the bear's big brown eyes, and the bear stared back.

"A friend?"

Gracie didn't really know what that meant. She heard her

brothers and sister talk about them and even her mama and daddy. Mama Darling said that the lady next door was her friend, so she guessed it was someone that smiled at you, talked to you, and brought you food sometimes. But Gracie didn't think this bear could smile, talk, or cook. She put down the needles and reached out and took the teddy bear.

"Hello you, I'm Gracie."

Something about the bear made Gracie smile. Even as slow as she was, she knew the bear couldn't talk. But there was something about the shine in his golden brown eyes; the way that they looked at her that made her think that even if he couldn't talk, he could listen.

"Maybe this is what a friend is," thought Gracie, "someone that listens and makes you feel good."

That night when Gracie went to bed, she took the teddy bear with her. She climbed under the cover with him under her arm. When her grandmother kissed her on the cheek and turned off the old seashell lamp by her bed, Gracie didn't go to sleep.

She turned to the teddy bear and said, "I don't know your name, but I'm going to call you Cookie Darling, because cookies are sweet and taste good. And darling must mean something really sweet and good like Mama Darling."

Then she told him all about her room and the little yellow bus and how to write her name, and she counted to ten for him. She told him lots of things that wouldn't really be important or interesting to anyone else. But they were important and interesting to Cookie Darling. He lay under Gracie's arm, warm under the old quilt in his new home, and his brown button eyes shone with love to every word that Gracie said. When Gracie finally drifted off to sleep, Cookie Darling was still wide-awake and still listening.

The next morning when Gracie's eyes opened, she could smell bacon cooking. She could hear Mama Darling humming in the kitchen. She could see blue sky out her window, and she could feel something fuzzy touching her cheek. When she rolled over, she was staring into the eyes of Cookie Darling.

"Well, hello there, Cookie Darling. Did you sleep good?" She swept up the teddy bear onto her chest.

"Do you smell the bacon? I like it real brown and crisp. Don't you?"

Then she rolled out of bed and pulled on her red and blue dress. She reached down and picked up her white socks with the daisies around the tops and slid in her feet. With Cookie Darling under her arm, she skated across the wooden floor out of her little bedroom and into the kitchen.

"Good morning, Mama Darling, from me and Cookie Darling." Gracie sat down in one of the mismatched vinyl chairs at the old walnut table. Her grandmother turned from the stove, skillet in hand.

"Gracious me, sweet pea. Good morning to you and your bear." Mama Darling chuckled as she slid the bacon out of the skillet onto a white plastic plate on the table.

"What did you say the bear's name was, Cookie Darling? That's a mighty fancy name for a bear."

"Well he's sweet like a cookie and I love him like I love you, so I thought Cookie Darling would be a good name."

Gracie wouldn't look up from the table. She wasn't so sure that she hadn't done something wrong.

"Baby, there's nothing wrong with the name and Mama Darling ain't mad at you. I guess I'm kind of flattered. I ain't ever had a bear named after me before."

Cookie Darling just sat on the edge of the table waiting. He had a worried look in his eyes. He wanted Gracie to be happy. So, he sat very still and listened very closely.

Gracie looked at her grandmother as she put a piece of bacon in her mouth.

"I'll take care of him, Mama Darling. He won't be no trouble to you."

Her grandmother sat down beside her and put her arm around her. "Gracie, if he makes you happy, he won't be any trouble at all. I just want you to have a friend, and if Mr. Cookie Darling here with the funny hat and scarf can be that to you, then he's more than welcome."

Her grandmother reached over and patted the bear on the head. Gracie stuffed another piece of bacon in her mouth, kissed her grandmother on the cheek, grabbed Cookie Darling from off the table, jumped up from her chair and ran out of the room.

"Come on Cookie Darling, I need to show you around."

Gracie took Cookie Darling back into her room. She showed him the flower that was growing in her window. It was an Africa Viola, or something like that. She showed him her closet with the six dresses she wore. She pulled each one out and asked him what he thought. Cookie Darling liked them all. He liked anything that was Gracie's. She showed him the yellow chest where she kept her socks and shorts and underwear. She showed him the beautiful angel that sat on the table next to her bed. Gracie told Cookie Darling that the angel was a special woman that watched out for her at night. She pulled out her flashlight and made it go on and off. Cookie Darling looked at Gracie with amazement. He was listening very hard.

"Now, Cookie Darling, my own friend, I want to show you my very, very own, very special things."

Gracie pulled a cardboard box from beneath her bed. Being a good detective, Cookie Darling held his breath with excitement. Being a good Cub Scout, he was polite and waited patiently. Being a good listener, he perked up his brown fuzzy ears.

Gracie pulled a stack of books and magazines out of the box. She showed the teddy bear each one of the books. The books were very worn and had obviously been looked at thousands of times. She told him a story with each book and showed him all the pictures.

When she picked up a magazine, she looked at Cookie Darling and said, "If you see something you like in one of these, I can cut it out for you. I cut out pictures for myself all the time."

When she held Cookie Darling over the edge of the box, he could see loose pictures in the bottom. There were pictures of children playing on the seashore. There were pictures of big houses with yards full of flowers. There were some cutouts of just faces or animals. Gracie took each picture out, held it to her chest and hummed a little song. Cookie Darling thought it sounded a lot like the one that Gracie's grandmother had been humming earlier that morning. Then Gracie hugged Cookie Darling so hard against her chest that he could hardly breathe.

"I'm so glad you're my friend. Let's go swing." And before Cookie Darling could even get his breath back, he was sailing out the back door with Gracie, and flying back and forth through the air in an old tire swing in the backyard.

Gracie's grandmother was hanging clothes on the line. "Goodness, child, you ain't been in that swing for years."

Then she chuckled, clicked her tongue against her teeth and stuck a clothespin on a tattered red bath towel.

All afternoon, Gracie and Cookie Darling played on the swing, looked at plants, lay on their bellies and watched ants march into their hills, caught a grasshopper, and listened to birds sing. All the while Gracie talked to Cookie Darling. He listened very closely and was amazed by all that she told him. Later that night when Gracie and her grandmother were sitting in their usual spots on the couch in front of the

TV, the teddy bear was sitting on her lap.

When she picked up her knitting needles she looked at her grandmother and said, "I want to make Cookie Darling something."

"Well, let's see child. He's got a hat and a scarf already. But he does not have a sweater. I think a sweater might look right nice on Mr. Cookie Darling. Wait just a minute here."

Then her grandmother reached over the side of the couch and pulled up her old knitting basket.

"I think I've got just the yarn for a nice little sweater."

She pulled out two wads of yarn, one blue and one white. Gracie looked at the yarn and then at her grandmother.

"You'll have to get me started."

And her grandmother did. She showed her how to loop over and under and through. Gracie kept going, occasionally looking at Cookie Darling and winking. He didn't wink back, but he wanted to. Mama Darling would stop Gracie and tie ends together. Then she'd show her another way to weave the threads and Gracie would be off and running until her grandmother would stop her again.

It took Gracie about three nights to finish the sweater. When she pulled the little blue and white sweater over Cookie Darling's head, it fit perfectly. Gracie beamed with pride. Her grandmother just chuckled and clicked her tongue against her teeth. Cookie Darling wished he had a mirror because he knew he was one good-looking bear.

That night in Gracie's room, Cookie Darling in his blue

and white sweater, detective hat on his head, and Cub Scout kerchief on his neck, lay snug under one of Gracie's arms. His brown button eyes were wide open as he marveled at all the things in Gracie's world. His brown fuzzy ears were at attention just in case Gracie's snores turned into words. He wanted to hear them all.

The next Sunday when Gracie's family came over for dinner, she didn't even mind when her sister asked who the crazy looking bear was. She didn't hear her mother say, "Poor little Gracie," and didn't notice her brothers playing games without her.

When Gracie finished dinner, she took Cookie Darling out to swing. When they got tired, they went into her room and Gracie showed him her books and told him stories. She didn't hear the car pull away from the house or the screen door slam as her grandmother came back in. She didn't pay any attention to the sounds of dishes and pans and hums as her grandmother cleaned up the kitchen. Gracie was busy with her friend. Gracie was happy. And Cookie Darling never took his eyes off her. Proud as a peacock in his new blue and white sweater, he sat on the edge of Gracie's bed, and not only listened, but listened with love in his heart.

Gracie had never been happier. For weeks, she spent every afternoon, evening, and weekend with Cookie Darling. She talked non-stop to him. Pretty soon, Cookie Darling could tell every story from Gracie's books he had heard them so often. Gracie had a friend, a good friend that really listened to her.

Then she met Trudie. Trudie was a new girl who appeared at school one morning while Gracie was in her favorite book corner. She had light brown frizzy hair and blue eyes. She had a big blue bow tied to her ponytail. She walked around with her head held down. She seemed to shuffle. And every time she was introduced to someone, she would hold out her hand without looking up.

When they brought her over to meet Gracie, Gracie was a bit perturbed because she was looking at one of her favorite books.

"Gracie, I want you to meet Trudie. She's new here and she needs someone to show her around."

Gracie said, "Hello, nice to meet you." She didn't look up from her book.

"Gracie, we thought you might show Trudie around the school."

Gracie set the book down on the table and looked up. At the same time, Trudie peered out from underneath her eyebrows with a nervous smile on her face. Gracie thought that Trudie must be close to her size. She also realized that Trudie was standing up, not lying on a mat or sitting in a chair.

"Okay, I guess I can do that."

Gracie stood up and took Trudie by the hand and said, "Let's go."

Gracie showed her where they ate their snacks and lunch. She showed her the little playground out back. She showed her the place where you could put on strange earmuffs and listen to either music or stories. And finally, she showed her the book corner, Gracie's favorite spot. All the time, Trudie never said a word, but she did seem to be smiling more.

When they called them for lunch, Trudie went with Gracie. The two girls sat there with their sandwiches and chips and looked at each other.

Finally, Trudie said, "Would you like to see my picture book?"

Gracie said, "Okay" as she nibbled off the end of her potato chip.

Trudie went to the cubby where they stored their backpacks and coats. She came back with a photo album and handed it to Gracie. When Gracie opened the album, she saw all kinds of pictures cut out of magazines, pictures of faces, and houses with flowers in the yards, and animals of all kinds.

Gracie said with excitement in her voice, "I cut out pictures too. I'll bring mine tomorrow."

When Gracie got off the bus that afternoon, her grandmother was sitting on the porch with Cookie Darling beside her. Gracie kissed her grandmother on the cheek and picked up Cookie Darling and gave him the biggest hug.

"There's a new girl at school and she likes books and she cuts out pictures and she can walk all by herself and she can talk and she is so smart that she can count to twenty-two."

Mama Darling clicked her tongue against her teeth and

chuckled, "Well, Cookie Darling, it seems that Gracie has a new friend."

Cookie Darling's eyes danced with joy. He liked to see Gracie so excited and happy. That night Gracie told him more about Trudie. She wasn't sure of her name but she knew all about how she looked and what she liked. She had Cookie Darling help her pick out pictures to take the next day to show her.

Pretty soon, Gracie and Trudie were inseparable at school. And one Saturday, Trudie's mother brought her over to Gracie's house. While Mama Darling and Trudie's mother talked on the porch, Gracie introduced Trudie to Cookie Darling.

"He is so cute!" Trudie picked him up and hugged him.

"I like his hat and scarf and sweater."

"I made the sweater myself," beamed Gracie.

She showed Trudie her plant and her window and her chest of drawers and her angel and her special box with all her books and pictures. She and Cookie Darling took her into the backyard and Gracie and Cookie Darling pushed Trudie in the swing.

Cookie Darling liked Trudie. She was nice and she made Gracie happy. So, hanging between the two girls, or sitting on Gracie's shoulders, or perched in Trudie's lap, his eyes were aglow with the newness of Trudie and the things that Gracie told her. And he did his best to sit still, so he could listen and hear everything.

Soon, Trudie was spending the night at Gracie's house or Gracie was staying at Trudie's. Of course, Cookie Darling was with them every time and he slept between them; sometimes squished or mashed under an arm or two, but he never complained. He just liked being with them and hearing all they had to say. They showed him all the pictures they cut out and he watched as Trudie helped Gracie make her own picture book. He was more than pleased and a bit full of himself when Gracie pasted a picture of a teddy bear on the cover of her book. They counted all the things they could find, sometimes loudly, and sometimes in whispers when they were told to hold it down a little. And Gracie, after all the years of being lonely and without friends, now had two friends.

One day at school they went on a special trip. It was to a swimming pool. Gracie and Trudie had to put on special clothes and wore these little things like rubber bands that pinched their noses. They were scared, but still laughed a lot, because they sounded so funny when they talked. Gracie really didn't want to get in the water, but when she saw Trudie climb in, she was right behind her. It was a strange feeling to her. In the water she didn't feel so heavy and slow. She seemed to be moving like those birds she saw outside of her window and in the backyard. She loved watching the bubbles that formed when she let out her breath in the water. And she laughed so hard, she thought she might use the bathroom right there in the pool when she and Trudie started splashing each other.

"I can't wait to tell Cookie Darling about this," she thought to herself.

Cookie Darling didn't know what a swimming pool was, but Gracie told him it was like the bathtub, only bigger, and he knew what that was from sitting on the edge while Gracie took her baths. He did know it made her happy. He could tell from her voice as he sat alert, fuzzy ears perked and listening.

Soon, Gracie wasn't always taking Cookie Darling to bed with her. She did talk to him, but it was less and less. She was always busy with Trudie. Cookie Darling began to spend more and more time sitting on the table beside Gracie's bed. He wasn't unhappy there. He could still see everything that went on in her room. And he liked it when Trudie came over because he could listen to all the words and stories they exchanged. Finally, one morning when Mama Darling was taking Gracie for a doctor's visit, Gracie picked up the teddy bear and one of her favorite books before she left.

At the doctor's office, Gracie was nervous, but Mama Darling kept her arm around her and Gracie kept her arm around Cookie Darling. When she finally got called into the doctor's office, he started by listening to her chest with a funny looking thing that was hanging from his neck. Then he tapped on her knees with a little thing that looked a lot like hammer. And finally, he tied a gray band around her arm. As he was doing these things, he kept talking to her about how her grandmother told him she was swimming, having fun in school, and that he understood she had two new friends. She began to feel just a little less nervous.

Pretty soon, he had Gracie laughing, especially when he held the thing around his neck up to Cookie Darling's chest to listen. When he finished, he gave Gracie a book to take home with her. She was so thrilled with the book and all its pictures that she forgot about Cookie Darling sitting on the examination table. Mama Darling didn't notice either as she was just proud that Gracie was all right, especially since her heart had always had a strange rhythm.

When they got home, Gracie had her grandmother call Trudie for her. Gracie could never remember the number. She wanted to tell her about the doctor. She wanted to tell her about the new book. She wanted to ask if Trudie could come over and look at the book with her and cut pictures out of the magazines her grandmother had gotten at church on their way home.

It wasn't until the next day that Gracie noticed Cookie Darling wasn't sitting on her bedside table. She thought to herself, "Now, where can that old bear be?" But just then, Trudie and her mother pulled up to take Gracie swimming.

It was at least a week later when she took out her picture book with the picture of the teddy bear on the cover that Gracie remembered to look for Cookie Darling. Gracie went onto the front porch where her grandmother was sitting hemming a new dress for Gracie's mother.

"Mama Darling, I can't find Cookie Darling anywhere."

Mama Darling clicked her tongue against her teeth.

49

"Come on, sweet pea, and I'll help you look for your friend."

They looked in the closets. They looked in the kitchen. They looked in the swing in the backyard. And they looked in Gracie's special box under her bed. Cookie Darling was nowhere to be found.

"Do you think he's hiding, Mama Darling?" Gracie asked as she tugged on a strand of her hair.

"I don't know, sweet pea. Maybe he's found another friend. You know you've got Trudie now and maybe someone else needed a friend like Cookie Darling."

"He's a good bear, and at least I know he's warm, wherever he is, in his sweater. And you know, Mama Darling, if Cookie Darling did nothing else, he always listened to me no matter what I said and he always liked my pictures. I wish I had given him one of my pictures."

Mama Darling put her arm around Gracie, clicked her tongue against her teeth, and chuckled. "He sure was a good bear, sweet pea. Why don't we call Trudie and see if she can come over and help us make cookies?"

And Gracie started thinking about cookies and how good they smelled and how good they tasted and how she couldn't wait to see Trudie.

There was a new nurse at Gracie's doctor's office. This nurse didn't know all the patients very well yet. When she went into the examination room to set up for the next appointment, she found a teddy bear on the table. He had a detective hat on his head. A Cub Scout kerchief was tied around his neck. And he was wearing a blue and white knitted sweater. She picked him up and put him on a shelf in the corner of the room, wondering who had left their bear, while she changed the paper on the table. It wasn't until a couple of weeks later that someone saw the bear on the shelf. Neither the receptionist nor the nurse knew who his owner was.

"What a strange looking little bear," the receptionist thought. "Now, who do you belong to?"

But Cookie Darling didn't answer. He just sat there in his strange attire, button eyes shining. The receptionist had the strangest feeling though. It was almost as if the little teddy bear's eyes were watching her every move and she wasn't sure, but she would have sworn that he was listening to every word she spoke.

"Well now, my little friend, I think I know the perfect place for you."

The next morning Cookie Darling was under the receptionist's arm, traveling down a long white corridor and heading for a new home in the children's ward of the local hospital. He peered out from under the brim of his detective hat. He wished the lady carrying him would straighten up his sweater and kerchief. He wanted to look his best. His button eyes glimmered with anticipation. His fuzzy ears were on point because he wanted to hear everything. He was a very good listener.

Toby and Dr. Bear

Toby was ten years old. He used to have jet-black curly hair. He used to play soccer. He used to have friends. But now as he lay in his hospital bed, he thought to himself, "I don't have anything."

Well, he first thought he didn't have "nothing", but remembered that Mrs. Dobbs said that was a double something or another and was not correct. He liked Mrs. Dobbs. She was his teacher and she had been to see him a few times, but she didn't stay long because she always seemed to be crying. Everybody seemed to be crying around him. Toby cried for a while, but not much anymore. He guessed he had cried out all the tears he had in his head. He did cry sometimes after one of the treatments. They made him feel so bad and sick at his stomach.

He rolled over and looked out the window. Through the cellophane pictures of Winnie the Pooh and Tigger, he could see lots of tall buildings. If he made his eyes squint he could just make out a small grove of trees, and beyond them what looked like a park. He wasn't sure, but there seemed to be little ants moving around. He knew the ants were probably people, maybe even kids. Maybe, they were playing soccer. It didn't really matter. He didn't care one way or another. His mother said it was the chemicals that made him feel this way. When she was there, she held him a lot and rocked him back and forth. She didn't talk to him much. She was usually too busy talking to his dad or the doctors that kept coming in and out of his room.

Toby couldn't exactly remember when he got sick, but he guessed it started that time when he was playing soccer. He had the ball and was driving down field when he got this awful pain in his head. He thought his head was going to split open. The next thing he remembered, he was sitting on the bench with his coach's arm around him. His face was all wet, so he must have been crying. The coach kept telling him it was all right. He said that it was okay to cry when you felt bad or were sad. Toby felt really bad. Tony and Glen and Robert were standing around him. They weren't laughing. So, Toby didn't feel bad about the crying.

Then his mother picked him up and drove him home. He didn't even know if they won the soccer game or not. She put him to bed and gave him some aspirin. He didn't wake up till the next morning and the headache was gone. He heard his mother telling his dad that it was probably a bug or something. Then he heard the front door close as his dad left for work.

When his mother came into the room, she brushed back her blonde bangs and put her hands on her hips, "Well now, little man, do we feel like going to school or not?" She swept down and picked up his soccer uniform from the floor and stacked it on top of his football shaped toy chest.

"I guess so," Toby mumbled as he rolled out of bed. He felt a little woozy, but his head wasn't hurting. He went in the bathroom, took his bath, put on his favorite pair of jeans, his "Soccer Really Kicks" tee shirt, and his new Air Jordans. When he went to school that day, his mother was standing on the sidewalk laughing and waving. She thought every-thing was fine. So did Toby.

The morning went fine. Tony told him they had won the game. "What was wrong with you?" he asked as they walked to the art room.

"A bug or something, I guess."

Mrs. Dobbs put her finger to her lips to remind them that there was no talking in the hall.

In art, they made clown faces using tiny pieces of paper. Mrs. Cooper, the art teacher, hung his on the wall. In social studies they made artifacts out of clay. He got tickled because Glen made his look like their soccer coach. Mrs. Dobbs came over and fussed at them, but he could tell she wasn't really mad because he saw her smiling as she turned her head.

It was during math, when they were working with their base ten blocks showing what big numbers really were, that he suddenly felt dizzy. Then he couldn't see the blocks on his desk and the pain started again. He didn't remember yelling out, but the next thing he knew Mrs. Dobbs was beside his desk holding him in her arms and he was crying because his head hurt so badly.

She took him to the nurse and they called his mom. His mother took him to the doctor. The doctor said that maybe he was having migraines or something like that, but he thought that's what bread was made from and he didn't understand why bread had anything to do with why his head hurt. Then he was home again in his bed where he slept all night and dreamed about clown faces and artifacts and clay soccer coaches and Mrs. Dobbs reading stories.

It wasn't until a couple of weeks later during soccer practice that the third headache hit. It hurt so badly that not only did he cry and scream out, but he got sick at his stomach, and though he didn't want to, he threw up all over the bag of soccer balls.

That was when they first took him to the hospital. That was when it all seemed to begin. They put him in this big round thing. He felt like toothpaste being squeezed through a tube. Just when he thought he couldn't stand it anymore, they pulled him out. The doctor told his mom it was to take pictures of his brain. Toby knew his brain was inside his head. He knew it was what helped him think and see and walk and talk. He didn't know how they could take a picture of it without a camera.

Later that day, his mom and dad came into his room. He could tell that both of them had been crying because their eyes were red and puffy. His mom sat on the edge of his bed and his dad looked out the window. The way he stood there made Pooh look like he was sitting on his dad's head. "Toby, honey, the doctors say that there is a tumor growing inside your head." Toby thought about the plants that were growing in the windows in his room at school.

"It's like a knot of something that is getting bigger. That's what is giving you headaches." His mom reached out and stroked the black curls out of his face. "They have to give you some medicine to help shrink the tumor. Then, they want to go in and cut it out." Two of the biggest tears Toby had ever seen rolled down his mother's face.

"You mean like they'll give me aspirin?" Toby's eyes were as big as saucers and he could hardly talk. "How will they cut it out? Will it be like a haircut?"

Toby's mom grabbed him and pulled him hard against her chest. He heard his father sob at the window. "My little man, my sweet little man, they'll be putting a tube in and putting medicine in it and then…" but she didn't finish. She jumped up and ran from the room.

She hadn't told him it would be a needle that stuck under the skin on his chest. She hadn't told him it would make him feel sick at his stomach all the time. She hadn't told him all his hair would fall out. She hadn't told him his friends wouldn't be able to come by and see him. She hadn't told him he wouldn't be playing soccer for a long, long time. He had days to think about it. He had days when he had never felt more alone.

And then one day, this lady brought in the strangest looking teddy bear. The bear had on a brown tattered hat with a bill on the front and the back. The lady said it was a detective hat. He had a Cub Scout kerchief around his neck. Toby knew what it was because he had been a Cub Scout for a while. And of all things, the bear was wearing a blue and white sweater! Toby couldn't remember ever seeing a bear in a sweater. Even though he told the lady thank you, he wasn't sure he wanted the bear. He felt a little old for teddy bears. But the more he looked at the bear, the more the bear seemed to be looking at him.

And the first time he spoke to the bear, he wasn't sure, but he thought the bear's little fuzzy brown ears seemed to perk up out from under his hat.

"What are you looking at, Dr. Bear? You must be a doctor bear since you're in a hospital."

What Dr. Bear was looking at was one sad lonely little boy.

"Well okay, if you must sit on my bed, then here." Toby reached out and picked up Dr. Bear and put him on his chest.

"Be careful now, you can't sit on my needle port. It's like on the space shuttle, but it's where they put medicine in to shrink the plant growing in my head."

Then Toby showed Dr. Bear where the needle and tube came out from under the skin on his chest. Dr. Bear's brown button eyes seemed to grow with wonder. He listened to every word that Toby said.

"It doesn't hurt too much. I do get a little sick when they put in the medicine though." Dr. Bear thought Toby must be the bravest little boy ever.

"I guess you are wondering where my hair went. It just fell out. Now, I don't have any. It doesn't matter though, because Dr. Mike said they would have had to shave it off before they cut the plant out of my head."

Dr. Bear had never known anyone with a plant growing in their head. "Dr. Mike's okay. He comes in sometimes and talks to me about soccer. He said he used to play when he was my age." Dr. Bear just sat very still. He didn't want to touch the needle port. He thought he liked Toby's slick head. He just liked listening to Toby talk.

That afternoon and night, Toby told Dr. Bear all about his soccer team. He told him about what it meant to be a forward. He told him about his friends Tony and Glen and Robert. He told him about Mrs. Dobbs and school. He told him stories about wading in creeks and catching crawdads with forked sticks. Dr. Bear could almost feel the little pinchers of the crawdads nipping at his furry legs.

Sometimes, Toby would just hug Dr. Bear and tell him he wasn't really that brave. He really was a little scared, but not to tell anyone. Dr. Bear thought they would have to shave all his fuzzy fur off before he would tell anyone what Toby told him. When the nurses came in and checked Toby's temperature, Dr. Bear lay under his arm and watched their every move.

That night when Toby finally fell asleep, Dr. Bear's head was on the pillow beside him. Dr. Bear's eyes were wide open. He felt like there might be a plant growing in his head under his detective hat, there were so many stories and things Toby told him going around and around. He thought he must have a real heart because it was busting at the seams, it was so full of love for the bravest little boy he had ever known. He listened to the sounds of the hospital, the carts rolling down the hallways, distant voices, the clatter of pans, the clinking of glass, opening and closing doors, but most of all he listened for Toby. If he woke up and wanted to talk, Dr. Bear wanted to be ready to listen.

The next morning when they hooked up the tube to the needle port to begin Toby's treatment, Dr. Bear's eyes were on their every move. He wanted to make sure they did everything right. And when they finished and Toby became ill, Dr. Bear didn't mind at all when some of it got on his fur, nor when the nurse wiped it off with the cold wet sponge. He was too busy nuzzling against Toby's cheek. He lay with his detective hat on his head, Cub Scout kerchief around his neck, warm in his blue and white sweater, willing all the love he had in his fuzzy body into the sick little boy that held him so tightly he could barely breathe.

Toby was still asleep when his parents were talking to Dr. Mike, but Dr. Bear was wide-awake. He heard Dr. Mike tell them that that had been the last treatment. It was time for the surgery. Dr. Bear watched while Toby's mom and dad hugged each other and cried. He would have cried too if he could, but he didn't. He didn't want to wake Toby up by getting his face wet. That afternoon, Toby's parents told him about the surgery. Toby didn't say anything. When they hugged him and stroked his bald head, he just lay limp like a rag doll except for the arm he held around Dr. Bear.

When they finally left, Toby sat up on the edge of the bed with Dr. Bear in his lap.

"If you make your eyes squint, Dr. Bear, you can see trees over the top of those buildings."

Dr. Bear couldn't make his eyes squint, but he thought he could see the trees.

"Those may look like ants, but they're really people. I think they're kids playing soccer. Look, Dr. Bear, I think that kid just scored a goal."

Dr. Bear pretended he didn't feel the back of his head getting wet.

"You can't have a plant in your head all the time, I guess."

Toby lay back down on his bed and pulled Dr. Bear on to his chest.

"I guess I am a little afraid." Toby's voice quivered.

Dr. Bear wished he could put his detective hat on Toby to

help him think good thoughts. He wished he could tie the Cub Scout kerchief around his neck, so he could be true and brave. He wished he could pull the blue and white sweater over Toby's head and arms to make him feel safe and warm. He wished the plant was in his head and not Toby's.

That night they gave Toby something to help him sleep. His mother and father slept on cots by his bed. Dr. Bear didn't sleep at all. He was still wishing too hard. He was listening for Toby's voice. He was listening for a miracle.

The next morning when Dr. Mike and the nurses came to get Toby, he had a surprise.

He said, "Toby, we need one more doctor for your surgery."

Then he reached out and hung a stethoscope around Dr. Bear's neck, right over the Cub Scout kerchief. Toby grinned, grabbed Dr. Bear, and gave him a big hug. Dr. Bear had never been more proud. He sat on a shelf in the operating room and watched their every move. He wanted to make sure that they were doing everything right.

When they finished and put Toby back in a bed, they laid Dr. Bear beside him. Dr. Bear was still wearing all his strange attire including the stethoscope that was dangling and glittering in the soft lights of the monitors by the bed. As usual, he didn't sleep a wink. He watched the nurses move in and out. He watched Toby's parents sit on the bed and hold Toby's hands. He thought about soccer games and crawdads. He listened so hard he thought his fuzzy brown ears might fall off. When Toby spoke, he wouldn't miss it.

When Toby spoke, he would hear every word. He would listen forever if it took it. He would listen with love.

So, it was no wonder that two days later when a small sound came out of Toby's mouth, it wasn't his parents that heard it. It wasn't Dr. Mike or one of the nurses. It wasn't Mrs. Dobbs who had come by several times. It was a brown fuzzy bear wearing a strange hat, a yellow scarf, and blue and white sweater. It was Dr. Bear, proud as punch with a stethoscope dangling from around his neck, fuzzy face pressed tightly to Toby's cheek that heard the sound. In all his years of listening, Dr. Bear had never heard a sweeter sound. He had heard a miracle.

Over the next few days, Toby was awake more and more. By his side the entire time was Dr. Bear. Dr. Bear watched while the nurses and doctors checked the bandages on Toby's head. He watched as they changed the strange bags that hung from poles by Toby's bed. He watched while they took his temperature and blood pressure. And when Toby would raise his head slightly and smile at Dr. Bear, Dr. Bear would smile back with his eyes.

When Toby could sit up, Dr. Bear was the first thing in his lap. He held the bear while he ate. He held the bear while he read books. He even held Dr. Bear when Mrs. Dobbs came by to read him stories. Mrs. Dobbs not only hugged Toby the last time she came, she also picked up Dr. Bear and gave him a big squeeze too.

Over the next few weeks, the nurses would put Toby and

Dr. Bear in a wheel chair and ride them out to a little court-yard behind the hospital. Toby would hold him up and turn him round and round while he talked about the trees and butterflies and the birds that fluttered in and out of the bird bath in the corner.

One time, Toby picked up a rock from the side of the sidewalk and told Dr. Bear, "This could be an artifact. We studied them in school. Someone long ago may have made it or used it."

Dr. Bear could feel the detective in him coming out. He wanted to know more.

Sometimes, they went to a big activity room where there were other children. Most of them had bandages just like the one on Toby's head. They didn't seem to smile much, but Toby always smiled and said hello. Dr. Bear hoped that all of them could feel the smiles he sent their way through his big brown button eyes. They painted pictures. Toby painted a picture of a strange little bear wearing a blue and white sweater, a yellow Cub Scout kerchief, a stethoscope around his neck, and a detective hat on his head. Dr. Bear looked at the picture with amazement. He would have cried if he could.

At night, Toby and Dr. Bear would lie in the hospital bed, and Toby would either read to Dr. Bear or they would watch TV. Dr. Bear didn't know which he liked better, hearing Toby read him stories or listening to Toby tell him what was happening on the screen where people were always moving around. He guessed he just liked listening to Toby talk.

Sometimes, after the nurse had come in for her final check of the night, Toby would put his finger to his lips to let Dr. Bear know he needed to be quiet and then they would turn the TV on with the sound real low. As the colors from the screen would dance across the room onto the bed, Dr. Bear would snuggle closer and closer under Toby's arm. If the movies were scary, Dr. Bear would slide as far as he could under the cover, so he couldn't see. And when Toby would finally go to sleep, Dr. Bear would lie there with his fuzzy face pressed tightly against the little boy's cheek and think how lucky he was to be lying next to this brave little miracle boy. He would listen to every sound. He would listen to the breaths entering and leaving Toby's body, but most of all he listened very hard just in case Toby woke up and needed someone to talk to.

The day that Tony, Glen, and Robert came to visit, Dr. Bear thought his stuffing would pop out he was so excited. The boys sat on Toby's bed and talked a mile a minute. They talked about soccer, and school, and Mrs. Dobbs, and how Tommy Jones had fallen off the jungle gym and broken his arm, and how Sue Wilson had sent Glen a love note, and how Tony had gotten in trouble for blowing milk out a straw in the lunchroom, and that Robert had a new dog bigger than he was, and how it felt to have a plant inside your head, and what it felt like to have it cut out.

Dr. Bear just sat very still. He wanted to hear every word. He didn't want to miss a single smile on Toby's face. When the boys had gone and Toby was asleep from all of the excitement, Dr. Bear's brown button eyes were still wide-awake from the wonder of it all. His brown fuzzy ears were a little sore from having listened so hard.

The next day, Dr. Bear listened when Dr. Mike told Toby's mom and dad that he could go home. Everything seemed to be fine. Dr. Bear watched as they hugged each other and Toby. Toby's mom even picked up and hugged Dr. Bear.

"Did you hear that Dr. Bear. I'm okay and I'm going home." Dr. Bear heard every word.

"You're going to like my house, Dr. Bear."

He held him in the air and twirled him around and then he stopped. A strange look crossed Toby's face. He thought about all the children in the activity room. A tear streamed down his cheek.

Toby looked up at his mom. "You know, Mama, I love Dr. Bear, but he really belongs here since he is a doctor and all. I have Robert and Glen and Tony and you and Dad. I don't think that some of the kids here have any friends. They need someone like Dr. Bear. They just need someone who listens.

Toby picked up Dr. Bear and gave him the biggest and hardest hug he could give and whispered, "Thank you, I love you."

Then, he sat Dr. Bear on the table by the hospital bed, picked up his soccer bag filled with his pajamas and socks and the picture of Dr. Bear, and walking between his mother and dad, he left the room.

Dr. Bear thought if he didn't have a heart before, he knew he had one now; and he hoped with all the fuzz that covered him, that the little brave miracle boy that just left could feel the love that he sent him from the bottom of his furry feet to the top of his detective hat.

When the attendant came in to clean the room later, he didn't notice the strange little bear sitting on the table. As he pulled the sheets from the bed, he didn't feel his arm brush the little bear off the table and into the garbage can. When he picked up the used bottles and bags and threw them into the garbage, he didn't see the top of the detective hat at the bottom. When he took the bag to the dumpster, he didn't know he had a very special passenger.

Dr. Bear's eyes were wide open with anticipation. His ears were pointed to hear every sound. Dr. Bear suddenly felt himself flying through the air. He heard a thump and the sound of plastic splitting. He began tumbling until he landed on the pavement on the street next to the hospital.

The next thing he knew there was a wet nose stuck in his face and a huge tongue that licked him from head to toe and he heard a voice say, "Whoa Sally, what is it girl?"

And then a baldheaded man with a beard was pulling a white dog back with a leash and reaching down and picking him up.

"What in the world? Good gosh, little bear, what are you wearing? Let's see, little fellow, you've got on a detective hat, and a Cub Scout kerchief, and a blue and white sweater, and even a stethoscope around your neck. You either are a jack-of-all-trades or you've seen quite a few adventures in your time. Well, my friend, I've got the perfect place for you. It looks to me like you've earned a rest."

As the man looked at the little bear he thought he saw a twinkle of light in his brown button eyes, and he had the strangest feeling that the little worn fuzzy bear, wearing the signs of many adventures, had heard every word.

Down the street the man walked with the white dog on a leash and Dr. Bear secured under his left arm. Dr. Bear's brown button eyes were wide with the newness of it all. And his little fuzzy ears were straining to hear every sound. After all, he was a very good listener.

Mr. Allen and Mr. Teddy

Mr. Allen was a school teacher. He wasn't married. He lived with a big white dog named Sally and a small black and white cat named Snake.

Snake got his name, not only from his black and white markings which looked a little snakelike on his face, but also from how mean and devilish he had been as a kitten.

He had appeared attached to the screen door on Mr. Allen's back porch one spring. When Mr. Allen opened the door, Snake held on with his claws. He was hanging on without his claws on the porch the next morning. And he continued hanging on there every morning after.

He found out later that Snake had belonged to a neighbor, and was named Pancake Kitty because they thought he would be run over on the busy city streets, and of course end up as flat as a pancake. Now, eight years later, Snake had had many brushes with danger and adventure, and had probably used up seven of his nine lives, but he was still hanging on at Mr. Allen's house.

Sally had once belonged to a friend. She came to stay at Mr. Allen's house for a while because he had a fenced-in backyard big enough for her to run and play. It had been almost a year and Sally was still there. As time went by, Sally seemed to spend more and more time in the house with Mr. Allen and Snake.

She did go out during the day and played with a dozen tug toys or throw toys or chew toys or items that had never been intended to be toys that had disappeared from the house. Mostly, she waited at the fence to hear Mr. Allen's truck turn in. Then she would bellow out a sound, somewhat like a barking seal in trouble or seeking its mate, to get his attention.

When he opened the front door, she was at the back, waiting to be let in. She would race through the house into the bedroom where she would grab his white socks lying on the carpeted floor and toss them into the air. She wanted Mr. Allen to put them on. She wanted him to put on his tennis shoes. Sally wanted to walk. She liked to strut down the street wearing her leash, with her ears perked, tail held high, and to smell all the smells of the neighborhood. It was on one of these walks that they happened onto the teddy bear.

Mr. Allen was very tired that day. It had been a long day at school. It had been one of those days when nothing went as planned. As he followed behind Sally down the street with the bear under his arm, he couldn't stop thinking about his day.

He worked in a resource room with special students. His students had trouble learning in one way or another for one reason or another. Some were wonderful in math, but struggled to read simple books. Others could read as fast as lightening, but numbers and what they meant were a mystery to them. Some of his kids couldn't sit still. Some couldn't learn as fast as everyone else. They just needed a little more time. They needed a little more attention. They needed a little more love.

Sometimes, Mr. Allen wasn't sure he had enough of whatever they needed to help them. Sometimes, Mr. Allen felt all used up.

The teddy bear bounced up and down under his arm. He felt nervous about this man who seemed on edge. His brown button eyes were wide-open and watching. His brown fuzzy ears were alert and listening.

Mr. Allen's morning had started with Jodie refusing to do her work. Jodie was a tiny girl with blonde hair, sharp as a new penny nail, but overactive and easy to unnerve or upset. Mr. Allen had to be careful when he corrected Jodie. She would become upset and sulk or sometimes even throw a tantrum in the middle of the room.

This morning she had thrown a tantrum. When he took her to time-out, she had called Mr. Allen everything, but a child of God. He had listened patiently and told her that when she could sit there quietly for five minutes, she could come back and work again. It took Jodie at least fifteen minutes to quit yelling and kicking. Finally, she called Mr. Allen over from his reading group and told him she was okay.

As usual, he put his arm around Jodie, asked her what choice had she made and why it was wrong. He asked her what she could have done differently. He told her he knew she could choose better, and then put her back to work. But Jodie did not choose better. She ended up throwing three more tantrums that day.

Then, there was Candy. She had just been put in Mr. Allen's classroom. Candy had short brown hair and big brown eyes. She couldn't read a lick, but could lick anyone that could read, no matter how big. Candy had learned to stand her ground. Maybe, she pushed other kids around because she was embarrassed that she couldn't read or write. Maybe, she hit and knocked them down because she didn't know any better.

When Mr. Allen worked one-on-one with Candy, he discovered that not only could she not read, she couldn't even put sounds together to make simple words. As he sat and worked with her and went over simple sounds and simple words again and again, he finally became frustrated.

After he told her she wasn't working hard enough and sent her from the table to think about it, he noticed she was crying. Then, of course, he felt badly and he had to give her his talk about how, "Nosiree Bob, nobody cries in this room because of work. You cry when you're sad or hurt. If you make a mistake you fix it. If you mess up you just try harder." But Candy cried anyway. Now, Mr. Allen felt like crying.

He backed off and thought. He took deep breaths and thought. He looked at Candy and thought. When he came back, he asked Candy if she wanted to read.

She wouldn't look up at him. She wiped her nose with a tissue. She pushed back her brown bangs and stared at the floor. Then, she nodded her head.

He told her he knew it was hard. It was going to be difficult, but if she tried her best she could do it and he would help her. Then he started all over and pretty soon, she read a couple of words and she was smiling. Mr. Allen was hugging her when another kid came to the door to tell Mr. Allen that Jodie was throwing another fit.

Mr. Allen unhooked Sally's leash from her collar. He sat down on the edge of the steps to his front porch. He had been thinking so hard about his day at school, he didn't even remember the last part of his walk. He didn't see the limbs of the trees waving over the sidewalk. He didn't feel the cool breeze as it blew across his face. He didn't hear the hellos of passing walkers or the barks of neighbor's dogs or even Sally's answers. As he weighed all that had happened that day, and the things he did or should have done or could do tomorrow, he forgot the teddy bear under his arm until he felt something fuzzy touching his leg.

"I forgot I had you there, little fellow." He picked up the bear and sat him on his lap.

"My mind is tied up around my kids. No, not my own kids, but my students at school."

He didn't know why he told the bear that. It was almost like he had answered a question.

The teddy bear sat still and didn't take his eyes off the tired teacher's face.

"I just want them to do their best. I don't like to see them get hurt. What about you little fellow? Where in the world did you get all these strange clothes, Mr. Teddy? I hope you don't mind if I call you Mr. Teddy. You look pretty proper in your hat and sweater and scarf and even wearing a stethoscope."

Mr. Teddy sat tall and straight like a statue. He had been a little nervous around the bald-headed man with the beard. He wasn't used to being around adults very much. But the more he listened to the man, the more he heard the sound of children's voices. The closer he sat to him, the more he felt the hugging arms of a hundred children. The more he looked into the teacher's eyes, the more he thought he saw the same twinkle he saw in children's eyes. Mr. Teddy suddenly felt very much at ease. And when the man smiled at him, though the smile looked weak and tired, Mr. Teddy knew it was weighted down with love.

Mr. Allen smiled at Mr. Teddy because he had the strangest feeling that the old bear was giving him the once over. There was something in those golden brown button eyes that seemed to ask who he was. There was also softness in the worn fuzzy fur that invited a hug, and for you to let go, like sinking into an overstuffed easy chair or cuddling under an old quilt. There was something about the pointed brown fuzzy ears and the way they stood alert like antennas. They seemed to catch every sound.

"You are a most unusual bear. For some reason, Mr. Teddy, I feel just a little bit better because you're here."

He hugged the bear as tightly as he could and rocked him to and fro. He felt like he was rocking his students. He was listening to Candy read. He was watching Jodie work. They were smiling and happy and Mr. Allen's heart felt full.

He would have continued to rock Mr. Teddy if the wet nose of a big white dog who was feeling a little bit jealous had not poked between the bear's face and his own.

"Sally, Sally. That's enough, girl. I'm just talking to our new friend here, Mr. Teddy."

Mr. Allen laughed and stroked Sally's head with his hand. He held the bear down in front of Sally.

"Mr. Teddy, this is Ms. Sally. Ms. Sally, this is Mr. Teddy."

Sally licked Mr. Teddy so hard she almost knocked his detective hat right off his head. Mr. Teddy had had lots of wet things on him before, but he couldn't remember anything like Sally's lick. Mr. Allen picked him back up and held him in front of his face.

"I don't know where all you have been, but you do look like you could use a rest. Children can sure use you right up if you're not careful. I think I've got the perfect place for you. Don't you think he'll like it on the bench, Ms. Sally?"

Mr. Allen held open the front door of his house while Sally loped by and then he swung through with Mr. Teddy on his hip.

Mr. Teddy was more than curious to find out what his new friend meant by a bench. Being the good detective, he knew he would soon find out. Being the good Cub Scout, he would be mannerly and polite to his new friends. In his blue and white sweater he would generate as much warmth and love as he could. With his stethoscope he would try to heal all the wounds Mr. Allen seemed to have and help him with his kids. But most of all, he would perk up his little brown fuzzy ears and listen.

In Mr. Allen's office was a park bench full of stuffed animals, not just any stuffed animals, but old ones with worn places and patches. Some were missing eyes. Others were missing an ear or a nose.

Mr. Allen held Mr. Teddy out in front of him.

"Mr. Teddy, here is your new home. I guess you wonder what all these old animals are doing here. I sort of collect them. I take them when other people throw them away. I figure that they have either given out so much love or have been loved so much that they are worn out and are no longer attractive to most people. But I think they're beautiful and deserve just a little bit of love, a little bit of peace and quiet, and maybe a place to rest. They don't deserve to be thrown away. Nobody deserves to be thrown away. We are all special in one way or another, just like you, little friend."

Mr. Allen's eyes seemed to mist over as he talked. There was a tugging at the corners of his mouth as he tried to smile.

Mr. Teddy thought he needed a handkerchief. He had never heard more beautiful words.

"Let me introduce you to everyone my new friend, Mr. Teddy."

And he did. Mr. Teddy met a monkey in a red boxing suit with no eyes wearing green plastic glasses. Mr. Allen had retrieved him from a box of garbage. The monkey looked like he had gone down for the count from too many hugs.

"Could you be knocked out from too many hugs?" Mr. Teddy wondered. He remembered being hugged so hard that he thought he might pass out.

There were two rag dolls in faded native costumes. Their faces were forever painted into smiles, though there was weariness in their eyes. They had been rescued from a yard sale. Whoever had owned them had kept them together. They had been carried so much that handprints were faded into their arms.

There were two small sock monkeys with bright red lips. A large gray sock monkey was missing his nose, but he still looked wise and stately sitting on the bench. He seemed to watch out for the little monkeys. He had probably always watched out for someone. Mr. Teddy wondered how he lost his nose.

There was a stuffed goose wearing a flaming red ribbon. She had a patch sewn on one of her wings. Mr. Allen had found her in a ditch by the side of the road. The poor goose had flown through the air for many a child. While they slept, she had perched on their pillows and helped their dreams fly right out the window and into the night sky.

A little brown teddy bear sat at the corner. His eyes seemed to dance and laugh though the bottoms of his feet were worn through to the stuffing. He came from a garbage can. He had been dragged so many places, he had traveled so many roads, and he had walked in so many children's tennis shoes that his feet were worn out.

In the teddy bear's lap sat a tiny duck in a billowy gingham dress with a crocheted collar. The little duck had called out to Mr. Allen at a flea market one Sunday during the summer. She had spoken of feathery dreams, and cool ponds, and lazy days, and the love of a child.

Mr. Teddy met them all. He felt quite princely in his sweater and scarf and hat and stethoscope. He felt almost new when he saw all their worn places and missing eyes and ears and noses. He was in awe of the sense of dignity and warmth and love that seemed to surround them. It was as if a light shone through them.

"Maybe that's what led Mr. Allen to find them," thought Mr. Teddy, "Maybe they had been involved in so much love that it glowed from them like a light."

When Mr. Allen sat Mr. Teddy on the bench, he felt

privileged to be sitting amongst them. He figured that these new friends had many a story to tell, many an adventure to share. He also thought Mr. Allen just might need for him to listen to more stories about school. He might need for him to help with his children. At the end of those long days when nothing went as planned, he might need a fuzzy hug.

Yes, Mr. Teddy was tired and he guessed he could use a little rest. But he sat alert and ready anyway. Between the sock monkeys and the goose, he posed in his blue and white sweater, a gift from a lonely little girl. He wore a Cub Scout kerchief like a small boy who couldn't talk very plainly and who missed his dad. Around his neck was a stethoscope to remind him of miracles and the bravest little boy in the world. On his head was an old detective hat and with it the memories of a twisting and turning girl who taught him that life is full of adventures and mysteries. Though he didn't know it, he also seemed to glow as if a light shone through him from all the love he had known and all the love he had shared.

As he sat there and watched Mr. Allen move around the room, he pushed his little fuzzy ears as far out of and above the hat as they would go. He strained with every ounce of fuzzy being he had. He wanted to hear anything and everything. After all, he was a very good listener. And sometimes, that's more than enough.

15335807R00050

Made in the USA
San Bernardino, CA
23 September 2014